ADVENTURES IN WILD SPACE

THE COLD

TOM HUDDLESTON

P R E S S

LOS ANGELES · NEW YORK

© & TM 2017 Lucasfilm Ltd.

All rights reserved. Published by Disney · Lucasfilm Press, an imprint of
Disney Book Group. No part of this book may be reproduced or transmitted
in any form or by any means, electronic or mechanical, including photocopying,
recording, or by any information storage and retrieval system,
without written permission from the publisher.
For information address Disney · Lucasfilm Press,
1101 Flower Street, Glendale, California 91201.
Printed in the United States of America
First United States Paperback Edition, October 2017
1 3 5 7 9 10 8 6 4 2
FAC-029261-17251
ISBN 978-1-368-00308-7
Library of Congress Control Number: 2016942982

Cover art by Lucy Ruth Cummins
Interior art by David Buisán

Visit the official Star Wars website at: www.starwars.com.

SUSTAINABLE
FORESTRY
INITIATIVE

Certified Chain of Custody
Promoting Sustainable Forestry

www.sfiprogram.org
SFI-01054

The SFI label applies to the text stock

CONTENTS

ADVENTURES IN WILD SPACE

THE COLD

*It is a time of darkness. With the end of the
Clone Wars and the destruction of the Jedi
Order, the evil Emperor Palpatine rules the
galaxy unopposed.*

*Since their parents were kidnapped by
Captain Korda of the Imperial Navy, Lina
and Milo Graf have fallen in with the rebels
Mira and Ephraim Bridger on the Outer Rim
world of Lothal. They have survived monsters,
aliens, gangsters, and ruthless bounty
hunters but are still no closer to discovering
the location of their mother and father.*

*When all hope seems lost, the Bridgers
receive word from spies within the Empire
who claim to know where the children's
parents are being held....*

CHAPTER 1
LINA'S LIE

THE SPEEDER bike's engine shrieked as it tore through the forest, its repulsors throwing up a plume of dead leaves and scraps of moss. Milo Graf thumbed the gears, pushing the speeder even faster. He turned sharply, almost ploughing straight into a greddleback termite mound the size of a Wookiee.

"Those things are everywhere," he complained, weaving around the nest.

"You'd see them sooner if you weren't going so fast," shouted his sister, Lina. She was perched behind him, her arms locked around his chest.

"Do you want us to get caught?" Milo shouted back, racing through a clearing. Lina squinted. She had become accustomed to the gloom of the forest, and the sudden light, unfiltered by the thick canopy, was blinding.

They disappeared back into the trees, almost crashing into the twisted trunk of a sprawling fallen tree.

"Any sign of them?" Milo asked his sister, spitting out an insect that had flown into his mouth.

Lina glanced over her shoulder. "No, I haven't seen them for ag—"

She broke off, spotting a flash of red through the fungi-covered tree trunks.

"There they are!"

Lina cried out as Milo swerved around a twisted hanava tree, nearly throwing her from the seat.

"Watch it!"

"You watch *them*!"

Keeping a tight hold on her brother, Lina

reached for the leather holster strapped to
her thigh. Unclipping a battered yellow energy
slingshot, she swiveled around, raising the
catapult. The scarlet speeder bike was gaining
on them, bobbing between the trees and
greddleback mounds. Its driver was hunched
over the controls, his face protected by a
mirrored mask. A slender figure sat behind him.
It was a woman, with a slingshot of her own.

The woman fired, a pellet of shimmering light

arcing toward them as Milo swung the speeder to the left. The shot went wide and burned up in the air, dissolving into a shower of small sparks. Lina exhaled in relief. That was close.

"What are you waiting for?" Milo called over his shoulder. "Shoot back!"

Closing one eye, Lina aimed the slingshot and fired.

The woman jerked back in her seat.

"I got her," Lina cheered. "I got her!"

"Finally!"

"I'd like to see you take a better shot!"

"Wanna trade?"

Before Lina could reply, Milo threw the speeder into a turn, the bike tilting so violently that Lina's kneepad scraped across the forest floor. She pressed herself against Milo's back and squeezed her eyes shut.

"Oh, no!"

Lina snapped her head up to look over Milo's shoulder. "Oh, no, *what*?"

And then she saw ahead the largest greddleback mound either of them had ever seen. It towered into the sky, as tall as a building! They were going to smash into it!

"Milo!" Lina screamed, but her brother didn't reply. He slammed on the airbrakes and the speeder jackknifed. It skidded sideways, straight toward the all-too-solid mound.

"Jump!" Milo yelled, flinging himself from the bike. Lina did the same, grunting as she hit the forest floor and rolled to a stop. The speeder pounded into the greddleback hill, sending dust and debris flying into the air.

"Mom's not going to be happy," Milo groaned as the red speeder bike screeched to a halt in front of them.

There was no escape this time.

Gingerly, Lina got to her feet, her hands raised in surrender.

"I'd get up if I were you," said the man in the mask as he swung himself off the speeder. His hand was already resting on his slingshot. "It's over!"

"You wish!" yelled Milo, scrabbling to his feet. "No surrender!"

He ran for the trees as their masked pursuer raised his slingshot and fired.

"Awww, not fair!" Milo groaned as the sensor plate strapped to his back buzzed. "Da-ad!"

The man reached up and pulled off his mirrored mask, revealing the handsome face of their father, Auric Graf.

"We won fair and square, kiddo!"

"Without crashing our speeder," the woman pointed out, glaring at them from the red speeder bike. Then she laughed, unable to keep up the act any longer. She got off the bike and hugged her daughter.

"Good shot, Lina."

Lina grinned up at her. "Don't worry, Mom. I'll fix Milo's speeder."

Rhyssa pulled Lina in tight. "I know you will. Like mother, like daughter!"

Behind them, Milo pulled out his comlink.

"Tell me you got all that, Crater," he said into the microphone. A mechanical voice responded immediately.

"*At the speeds you were traveling?*" said CR-8R, the Grafs' uppity droid. "*The holo-drones don't have hyperdrives, you know.*"

"He got it," said Auric, ruffling Milo's hair. "We can watch it together when we get back to the *Bird*. Let's go home."

"Pause!"

The image of Auric and Milo froze, the tall man gazing down at his son with affection.

Sitting in the *Whisper Bird*'s living quarters, Milo sighed. He must have watched the holo-feed a thousand times. That had been a good day. The best. Speeder tag through the termite forest of northern Indoumodo. His eyes played across the holographic scene in front of him. Mom helping Lina pull their crashed speeder back onto its repulsors. Milo laughing at Dad.

Mom had modified those slingshots herself,

the energy pellets harmless balls of light set to trigger the sensors strapped to their backs. Mom and Dad had always tried to find time for a game no matter what planet they were exploring.

Tears pricked Milo eyes and he sniffed hard. No, he wasn't going to cry again. That was not why he'd been browsing the Grafs' collection of holo-recordings. He just wanted to remember what life had been like before this nightmare had begun, before Mom and Dad had been kidnapped by Captain Korda of the Imperial Navy.

He would never admit it to Lina, but sometimes Milo struggled to remember what their parents even looked like.

"Shut down," he told the projector, and the forest scene vanished.

The *Whisper Bird*'s cramped living quarters had never seemed so empty.

A small rust-colored animal scampered

across the floor, squeaking happily as it threw itself into Milo's arms.

"Watch it, Morq!"

Milo laughed as his pet Kowakian monkey-lizard knocked him off balance. He rolled onto his back and hugged the creature. Somehow Morq always knew when Milo needed a pick-me-up.

"Come on," Milo said, prying the monkey-lizard's spindly arms from around his waist. "Let's go annoy Lina and Crater."

"Bringing us out of hyperspace."

The *Whisper Bird* shuddered as the swirling blue vortex outside the ship was suddenly replaced by a vast star field. Planets and moons rushed toward them and then stopped as the *Bird*'s sublight engines brought them to a halt.

Lina sat back in the pilot's chair and looked at the warning light that was flashing above her head. She reached up and tapped the bulb. A rear stabilizer was on the fritz. That wasn't a problem. Repairs could wait until they got back to Lothal. After everything the *Whisper Bird* had been through over the past few weeks, it was a wonder the old ship could fly at all, let alone navigate hyperspace.

Behind her, Milo burst into the cockpit. He was barely through the door before Morq leapt from his shoulder to land on CR-8R's metallic head.

"Get off me, you revolting fleabag," the droid snapped, swatting at the monkey-lizard with a chrome-plated arm. Lina grinned. Morq loved tormenting poor CR-8R, and despite his complaints, she had a sneaking suspicion that the droid secretly enjoyed the attention.

"Are we there yet?" Milo asked, flopping down in the chair behind CR-8R's navigator station.

"Yup," Lina said, avoiding looking her

brother in the eye. She busied herself with the fault locators. "Just need to check the primary systems before we locate the transmitter."

"I'm still amazed the Bridgers agreed to this mission," CR-8R said, finally dislodging Morq with a blast of compressed air from one of his many manipulator arms. "Entrusting the repair of a relay station to a couple of children . . ."

"Hey!" Lina said. "We know what we're doing!"

"Well, *you* do," admitted Milo. "I wouldn't know one end of a transmitter array from the other."

Lina rolled her eyes. She and her brother had been living with Ephraim and Mira Bridger on Lothal for a while, ever since they had been rescued from a traitorous bounty hunter known as the Shade. The Bridgers were rebels, secretly broadcasting anti-Imperial messages across the Outer Rim. They used a network of forgotten transmission satellites from the days of the Old Republic, hijacking frequencies the Empire considered obsolete. One such satellite had stopped functioning, and Lina had volunteered to travel out there to fix the problem.

"We're not sure," Mira had said, fixing the children with her purple eyes, but Lina could be extremely persuasive when she wanted to be.

"It's fine," Lina had told their hosts. "The transmitter's in the middle of nowhere, as far from the Empire as you can get. We can be there and back in just a few days. Besides, we'll have Crater looking after us."

She could still hear CR-8R's haughty response to that: "Mistress Lina, I was constructed by your mother to assist in serious scientific research. I am not a babysitter!"

The Bridgers had finally agreed. Lina's stomach tightened when she remembered Ephraim persuading his wife to let them go. "We can trust them, Mira. They know what they're doing."

Mira had sighed. "I guess you're right. We

can't expect them to stay cooped up in our basement forever."

Milo leaned forward in his chair to peer through the cockpit's transparisteel window. "So, how long before we get to Pion?"

Beside Lina, CR-8R turned at the name. "Pion? We're not going to Pion, Master Milo."

Lina closed her eyes and waited for the inevitable. This had been sure to happen sooner or later.

"Yes, we are," Milo insisted. "That's where Ephraim said we'd find the faulty transmitter. The Pion system."

Lina felt CR-8R's optical sensors boring into her. "But Mistress Lina told me to set course for the *Xala* system."

"The Xala system?" Milo repeated. Now he was staring at her, too. "Lina, you didn't!"

"Didn't *what*?" CR-8R asked.

Lina sighed. It was time to come clean. She swiveled in her chair to face Milo.

"The Xala system isn't that far from Pion. We can check here first and then head for the transmitter before the Bridgers even know what we've done."

CR-8R's arms were crossed across his barrel-like chest. "And what exactly *have* we done, Mistress Lina?"

"We've lied to the Bridgers, that's what!" Milo answered. "Well, *she* has!"

"Look, Crater," Lina began, "I didn't lie. I just didn't tell them we were coming here first. You remember that lead Mira got from her contact

in the Empire? The intel about where Mom and Dad are being held?"

"Intel?" CR-8R exclaimed. "Who do you think you are, Mistress Lina? A Bothan spy?"

"The information suggested they were being kept in the Xala system," Lina continued, ignoring the droid. "Here!"

"But Ephraim decided it was too dangerous," Milo reminded her. "There's no way of knowing whether the information's genuine or not. It could be a trap."

"Or it could be real. Ephraim was right. We don't know for sure unless we look. We can't just ignore it, Milo. If Mom and Dad are here . . ."

"No!" CR-8R said firmly. "You tricked the Bridgers. You tricked *me*."

"But, Crater—"

"No buts! I'm setting course for Pion this minute. Once the satellite is repaired, we're heading straight back to Lothal so you can apologize!"

Behind them, Milo sniffed. "Well, it wouldn't

hurt to have a quick look around would it? As long as we're here . . ."

CR-8R's head snapped around. "Master Milo! Not you, too."

"It won't take long, I promise," Lina said, seizing the moment. "We'll scan the system for life signs, that's all." She glanced out of the cockpit at the giant icy moon in front of them. "We'll probably find nothing, but if there's a chance Mom and Dad are out there . . ."

She let the sentence hang in the air. CR-8R looked from one child to the other before admitting defeat. "Oh, fine. But we're leaving at the first sign of trouble."

Lina didn't wait for him to change his mind. She fired the ship's engines, sending them flying toward the ice moon. "Thank you, Crater. You won't regret it, I promise."

The words were barely out of her mouth before an explosion ripped through the *Whisper Bird*.

CHAPTER 2
MOONFALL

"WHAT WAS THAT?" Milo cried out as he was thrown from his seat.

CR-8R checked the damage report. "We've been hit by blaster fire. Near the exterior heat vents."

Further explosions rumbled through the ship, the cockpit reeling as the *Whisper Bird* shook violently.

"More blasters?" Lina yelled.

"Negative," CR-8R replied, data flowing from the *Whisper Bird*'s computers into his own processors. "The initial shot has set off a chain reaction within the ship. We've lost the hyperdrive, fuel stabilizers, acceleration compensators. . . ."

The explosions kept coming.

"Can't you hold her steady?" Milo asked, trying to pry Morq from around his neck.

"What do you think I'm trying to do?" Lina snapped back, wrestling with the controls. "Who fired on us?"

"Hang on," Milo said, dragging himself back into his chair. Turning to the rear control panel, he flicked a large green switch. "The exterior scanners aren't working!"

"Why not?" Lina asked.

"How should I know?" Milo said, slamming his fist against a blank display screen.

"Allow me," CR-8R said, inserting a probe into the console's access port. It whirred and clicked as the droid tried to reboot the *Bird*'s communication system.

"Hurry up!" Milo said.

"I am!"

Static burst across the display, replaced a second later with the view from the back of the *Whisper Bird*. A sleek starship was on their tail. It was the color of a TIE fighter, with a long arrow-like hull supporting twin engines.

"Curious," CR-8R commented. "I've never seen a ship with that configuration before."

"It has to be Imperial," Milo said.

"This far into Wild Space?" Lina asked, still fighting to keep the *Whisper Bird* flying straight.

"I knew it was a trap!" CR-8R shouted. Another explosion rumbled through the ship, and Lina cried out as sparks burst from the controls above her. The ship lurched to the right, and Milo whacked his head on the computer console.

"Are you okay?" Lina shouted over her shoulder.

"I'll tell you when the room stops spinning," he groaned.

Lina yanked at the control stick, but nothing happened. "No, no, no! This isn't good!"

"What isn't?" Milo said, appearing at her side.

"The engines aren't responding," Lina said, frantically flipping switches on the dashboard. "I can't slow us down."

"How is that a problem? Shouldn't we be running away as fast as possible?"

"You don't understand," Lina said, looking through the canopy. "We're caught in the ice moon's gravity. We're going to crash!"

<hr>

On the flight deck of the Imperial ship, pilot droid RX-48 slammed his cracked blue visor over his electronic eyes in frustration.

"You were only supposed to disable their engines!" growled a deep voice behind him.

"Mission accomplished," RX-48 sneered as the *Whisper Bird* careened toward the

mountainous moon. "I also knocked out their navigation systems, life support, and deflector shields! Yay me!"

RX-48 could imagine the look on the humanoid's face. He could also imagine the idiot's hand reaching for his blaster.

Go ahead, the droid thought. *Blast me into a thousand pieces. I'd like to see you pilot the* Star Herald *on your own, you pretentious nerf herder!*

"Is something amusing you?" his employer snarled.

"Only that you stole a top-of-the-line Imperial scout ship to chase down that bucket of bolts," RX-48 replied. "Talk about overkill. What a junk heap!"

"That junk heap contains precious cargo. You'll be laughing on the other side of your vocabulator if it's destroyed."

RX-48 peered through his grimy visor. The *Whisper Bird* was in a bad way. Energy crackled across its engines, the glow of a dozen fires showing through cracks in its hull. There was no guarantee the ship would even make it to the moon, let alone crash.

"You said you were the best of the best," the droid was reminded by that grating voice. "Do something!"

"I said I was the *cheapest* of the best," RX-48 said, grabbing controls with all three of his arms. "You get what you pay for, sunshine!"

RX-48 heard the creak of his employer's leather gloves. Yup, the loony had definitely grabbed his blaster this time.

"But no need to get your medals in a twist," he added before his employer could permanently terminate their contract. "We'll catch them, just you wait and see. Engaging tractor beam!"

"That planet's definitely getting bigger!" Milo said, staring over Lina's shoulder.

"It's a moon!" CR-8R corrected, not looking up from the computer.

"I don't care what it is," Milo snapped. "Just stop us from hitting it!"

"The controls are dead," Lina said as a fiery glow spread across the canopy. "We're entering the atmosphere."

Milo didn't know what was worse, the heat in the cockpit or the horrible smell of burning.

There was a dull clunk from above, and yet

another alarm joined the chorus of electronic wails.

"What now?" Milo asked.

"The Imperial ship is attempting to lock on a tractor beam," CR-8R told him.

"Hooray for the Empire," Milo said with little humor in his voice. "Then why aren't we slowing down?"

Lina checked her instruments. "There's something in the moon's upper atmosphere that's scattering the beam. They can't get a fix."

"Great. We can't even rely on the bad guys to catch us. Any other ideas?"

Lina set her jaw, staring straight ahead.

"You won't like it."

"Try me," Milo replied.

She pointed at the ridge of snowy mountains that lay straight ahead. "We use them to slow us down."

Milo's eyes went wide.

"Use them how? We crash into them?"

Lina shrugged. "Or *bounce* off them."

"You're right. I don't like it," Milo told her. "Not one bit."

"What other choice do we have?"

Milo racked his brain. "Escape pods?"

CR-8R glanced at the fault locators. "Damaged beyond repair. We'll never launch them in time."

"Rocket packs?"

Lina shot him a look. "Are you crazy?"

"Says the girl who wants to use an entire mountain range as a crash mat!"

"Arguing is not the answer," yelled CR-8R. "Neither is plummeting into an ice planet, I'll admit, but—"

"Thought you said it was a moon!" Milo pointed out.

Lina swallowed hard. The mountains were getting closer by the second. "Okay, guys, brace yourselves. This is going to hurt!"

"What happened to the tractor beam?"

"I'm a little busy right now," RX-48 replied, using all three arms to control their descent. "Unless you want to take over?"

"An excellent idea!" his client said, appearing beside RX-48. Sliding into the copilot's seat, he swatted one of the droid's arms out of the way and took control of the vessel.

"Hey!" RX-48 complained. "Where are your manners?"

"They're weighing the pros and cons of pushing you out of an airlock!" The droid's employer narrowed his eyes, staring at the viewscreen. "Now what's happening?"

The view outside had been obscured by swirling clouds.

RX-48 checked his display. "Blizzard. Quite a doozy by the look of things."

"A little warning would have been nice!"

"It came out of nowhere," RX-48 insisted, flipping up his visor to stare hopelessly ahead. "I'm a pilot, not a weathervane."

A light flashed on the console.

"What's that?" asked the humanoid, glaring at the bulb as if it were the cause of all his problems.

"Proximity alert," RX-48 replied. "Remember those mountains, the ones covered in snow?"

"Where are they?"

"Your guess is as good as mine, but I'd pull up if I were you."

"What?"

"Unless you want to see what happens when a scout ship flies into a massive lump of rock!"

With a bellow that would make a Gamorrean blush, RX-48's thug of a boss yanked back on the controls.

"Are you sure about this?" Milo shouted as the *Whisper Bird* hurtled through the storm.

"I was," Lina admitted, "when I could still see where I was going!"

"Next time, I'm flying the ship!" CR-8R

moaned as pressurized steam burst from a pipe above his head.

"Who says there will be a next time?" Lina asked, holding what little was left of her nerve. "Here we go!"

Hoping she was doing the right thing, Lina pulled back sharply on the control stick. The *Whisper Bird* quaked, its nose slowly rising as the front repulsors fired. Flying blind, Lina had guessed the distance to the mountains. But had she guessed right?

There was a bone-shattering jolt as the ship struck something. Lina's head snapped back, and for a second she saw stars before she was thrown forward again.

Wham! There was another crash, followed by the sound of tearing metal, and they were flying straight again.

"We did it!" Lina shouted in relief, gripping the steering column.

"Did what, exactly?" CR-8R asked.

"Skipped off the top of the mountain,"
Milo said, breathing hard. "Like a stone on the
surface of a lake. You're amazing, Sis. A maniac,
but amazing all the same."

"Only if I can land us safely," Lina said,
peering through the snow. "We've leveled off,
but there's no telling what we'll hit when we
reach the ground."

Beside her, CR-8R's head whirred. "Accessing

Graf family records," he announced before pausing for what seemed like an eternity.

"Well?" Milo asked.

"Your mother and father never surveyed this moon," CR-8R finally reported. "Although a long-range scan indicated that about 89.94 percent of its surface is covered by frozen oceans."

Ahead of them, the blizzard had started to clear to reveal a vast expanse of ice stretching in all directions.

A vast expanse of ice that was getting closer by the second.

"Hold on to something," Lina said through gritted teeth. "I'm bringing her down!"

CHAPTER 3
CRASH LANDING

THE SOUND of the *Whisper Bird* hitting the frozen sea echoed across the barren landscape. The ship skidded, cutting a deep trench in the ice, before finally coming to a stuttering halt. Smoke billowed from its engines as the storm passed overhead. For a moment all was still, the arctic wasteland silent except for the distant cry of flying reptiles.

With a hiss of hydraulics, a hatch flipped open to clang loudly on the top of the stricken spacecraft. Lina Graf hauled herself up through the opening, pulling the collar of a thick winter jacket close around her neck.

"It's freezing," she said into her comlink.

"Tell me something I don't know!" Milo replied on the other end of the line. *"What's the damage?"*

Lina stood on the top of the *Whisper Bird* and looked around. The frozen ocean stretched as far as she could see, the desolate view broken up by a dozen or so forbidding islands. In the distance, vast plumes of water burst into the sky like geysers. It must have been the pressure of the sea below, pushing through the icy crust and up into the atmosphere.

They couldn't have landed on a more inhospitable snowball if they'd tried!

But standing around wasn't helping. The ice around the ship was littered with debris and hull plates scattered by the crash. The *Whisper Bird* was in pieces, but at least they had made it down alive.

"Lina?"

She raised the comlink to lips that were

probably turning blue. "Sorry. It could be a lot worse. What about in there?"

"The cockpit looks like it's been hit by a solar flare, and Crater's racing around like a dopplefly putting out fires. But other than that . . . fine."

"I'm going to look at the landing gear," Lina told him, starting to make her way down a ladder. She stopped at the final rung and jumped down onto the ice.

Lina's feet slipped out from beneath her and she landed with a *whumph* on her backside.

"Are you okay?" Milo asked.

Lina was glad he hadn't seen her fall.

"Fine! Just fine."

Sighing, she reached inside her jacket pocket and found a set of ice grips for her boots. She put them on before searching for gloves.

Spotting something, she gingerly rose to her feet. The spikes on her boots held. Good. She'd had enough crash landings for one day!

Sparks were cascading from the tip of the *Whisper Bird*'s starboard wing. Lina worked her way along its length, finding an exposed power cable. Instinctively, she reached for her tool belt. A damaged cable was the least of their worries, but repairs had to start somewhere.

"*Can I come out there with you?*" Milo whined over the comlink. "*Crater's driving me crazy!*"

"*Yes, please do,*" she heard CR-8R respond. "*Anything to get you from under my feet!*"

"*You don't even have any feet!*"

"We don't have time for this," Lina snapped. "That ship's still out there somewhere, remember?"

Milo's voice sounded sulky. "*Okay, just don't be long, all right?*"

Lina pulled out a pilex driver and started work on the wing. "I just need a minute to fix this—"

A deep groan stopped her from completing her sentence.

"*Lina?*"

What was that? An animal? No, it sounded structural, like the ship's hull creaking under pressure.

"*Lina, are you there?*"

There was a rumble beneath her feet, something she felt rather than heard. It vibrated through the ice, through the spikes on her boots, through her entire body.

Milo's voice came over the comlink. "*Lina, can you feel that? Is it a quake?*"

No, Lina realized, it was much worse than that.

"Milo, get out of there!" she screamed into the comlink. "Get out of there now!"

"*Why? What's—*"

She didn't hear the rest of the question. The ice beneath the *Whisper Bird* shattered as a column of steaming water erupted high into the sky. Lina was flung clear of the ship and thudded down on the ice, crying out in pain.

She slid to a stop. Water was falling like hot rain, sizzling against the ice, the same water that had thrown the *Bird* into the air.

The thought brought her back to her senses. The *Bird*!

Her bruised body ached from her fall, but she had to see. She scrabbled around, a sob of despair escaping from her chest.

There was no sign of the *Whisper Bird*. Instead, the ship had been replaced by a yawning hole in the ice.

"Milo!" she screamed, but it was useless. He wouldn't be able to hear her now.

The *Whisper Bird* had plunged into the depths below, taking Milo with it.

The deck pitched beneath Milo's feet and he took a nosedive across the cockpit. Somewhere above him, Morq gave a frightened yelp as loose panels and circuitry crashed down.

"It's okay, Morq," Milo called out, but he knew it wasn't.

One minute they had been on the ice, the next they'd been thrown into the air as if whacked by a giant graviball bat.

It had all happened so fast. The cockpit flipping upside down. Milo cartwheeling head over heels. Then there was the second impact, accompanied by a splash.

Milo had landed on his back, staring up at the water on the other side of the canopy.

Now there was another noise, a deep throaty rush of water somewhere from the back of the ship. For a moment, Milo couldn't tell where it was coming from, or what it meant. Then he realized.

The hatch. Lina had opened the hatch to get out. Freezing seawater was pouring into the living quarters. They were being flooded!

"Master Milo," CR-8R shouted, appearing at the cockpit door. "We're taking on water. It's the—"

"Hatch, I know," Milo interrupted, grabbing hold of a chair and pulling himself up to the computer terminal. "Can we close it from here?"

"No," CR-8R said. "It can only be closed by hand."

"Why am I not surprised?" Milo groaned as icy water cascaded into the cockpit. He gasped as the deluge hit him, taking his breath away.

"Climb onto me," CR-8R instructed.

"Why?" Milo spluttered in response.

"Just do it!"

Milo didn't wait to be told again. He clambered onto CR-8R's back, two of the droid's manipulator arms swiveling up to lock him in place. With a squeal, Morq jumped down to land on CR-8R's head.

"No, not you!" the droid protested.

"He's scared!" Milo insisted.

"So am I! Hold on!"

His repulsors complaining, CR-8R pushed against the tide of water. They reached the living quarters, briny seawater pouring through the open hatch high above. The room was filling up fast, and CR-8R was struggling to stay above the rising water levels.

"Get me to the ladder," Milo said. "I'll climb up to the hatch."

"You'll never make it," CR-8R told him. The droid hovered near a plastic storage barrel that was bobbing around in the churning water. His manipulator arms released their grip around Milo.

"You want me to get on that?"

"And take the monkey-lizard with you!" CR-8R said.

Milo swung his leg over the barrel, as if he were mounting a dewback. The plastic was slippery, and Milo had to grab the edge as Morq hopped onto his shoulders.

"What are you going to do?" Milo yelled above the roar of the water.

CR-8R didn't waste time replying. He fired his repulsors, rising toward the hatch. Milo wiped wet hair from his eyes as the droid all but disappeared into the torrent, mechanical arms gripping the ladder for support.

"Crater!"

The barrel was floating higher and higher, the water level almost up to the ceiling.

"Crater, are you okay?"

There was a creak and a slam, and the water stopped rising. Milo looked up to see a dripping CR-8R hanging from the ladder, the hatch closed tight above his head.

"You did it!" Milo cheered.

"My joints will be rusted solid," the droid responded, shaking his head like a musk-hound after a bath. "I've got water in my audio receivers, I just know it."

"Milo?"

Lina's voice crackled from Milo's waist. He grabbed for the comlink, his fingers stiff with the cold.

"Lina! We're here. Can you hear us? Repeat: can you hear us?"

"Barely," came the reply. *"You're breaking up."* Lina's voice was swamped with static, her words almost indecipherable.

"What was that? Lina, are you there?"

"I said hold on. I—"

And then she was gone.

"Lina! Lina, come in," Milo begged, shivering in his wet clothes. "Please!"

"Milo!"

Lina shook the comlink, as if that could help. Her brother's distorted voice had cut off, the signal lost.

Tears spilled onto her cheeks, instantly freezing in the driving wind. A storm was blowing up again. Lina stared into the gaping hole in front of her.

The *Whisper Bird* was gone, just like that.

There was no way of telling how deep the sea was beneath the ice. And even if she knew, what could she do about it? She was just one girl, standing alone on a frozen moon with only ice grips and a thermal jacket to her name. It was hopeless.

"Shut up," she told herself. "Milo's alive. You heard him. And Crater's down there with him.

They'll find a way. They'll fix the *Whisper Bird* and fly back to the surface. They just have to."

Something rumbled in the air. *Engines.* Lina turned to see a dot on the horizon. She pulled a pair of macrobinoculars from her tool belt and raised them to her eyes.

A terrified whimper escaped her lips.

The Imperial ship was racing toward her like a glistening bird of prey.

She let her arms drop, the macrobinoculars shaking in her hands. She didn't need them anymore. The ship was getting larger by the second. They'd shot the *Whisper Bird* down and were coming back to finish the job. She felt rooted to the spot, unable to move, unable to look away.

No! That's what they wanted. That's how the Empire won. By scaring people. By making them feel powerless. Milo wouldn't give up, and neither would she.

Lina looked around, her eyes settling on the

nearest island. Perhaps there *was* somewhere to hide. She took a closer look with the macrobinoculars. Yes. The rocks were pitted with caves. She had no way of knowing what was inside, but she'd have to risk it. Better to find a hiding place than stay out in the open like a sitting pelikki.

Lina started to run.

The island was nearer than she'd thought, but running in the cold air was almost impossible. Lina's muscles cramped and her lungs felt as though they were going to explode at any moment. Only the approaching roar of the Imperial engines propelled her on.

Reaching the rocks, she clambered up to a cave, the spikes on her boots scraping against the frozen ground. She fell once, grazing her knee through her thick trousers, but there was no time to check the injury. The Imperial ship had already landed a safe distance from the hole in the ice. Had they seen her?

Ducking behind a large boulder, she trained the macrobinoculars on the ship. Its hull gleamed in the cool sunlight, steam rising steadily from its heat vents.

As Lina watched, a ramp lowered and a tall figure swaggered onto the ice.

Lina's breath caught in her throat.

It couldn't be . . . could it?

The man had changed since she'd last seen him on Thune. The crisp Imperial uniform had been replaced by heavy body armor covered by layers of thick furs. His blonde hair blew in the arctic wind, no longer tucked neatly beneath a peaked cap, and his cheeks were unshaven, covered by many days of growth.

But even in that disheveled condition, there was no mistaking his identity.

Those hate-filled blue eyes.

That cybernetic jaw.

It was a face that she'd never forget, a face that haunted her nightmares. Captain Korda of the Imperial Navy. The man who had kidnapped her parents.

CHAPTER 4
THE FINAL HUNT

"WELL?"

Korda swore under his breath at the sound of RX-48's shrill voice, somehow even more irritating over the comm-channel. He snatched the receiver from his belt and barked a reply.

"Well *what*?"

"*Find anything?*"

A vein throbbed in Korda's temple. RX-48's insubordination was really beginning to grate. Not that long before, he would have had the pilot melted down for scrap, but now . . .

He stalked toward the edge of the ragged hole.

"You think it went through the ice?" RX-48 asked.

"Do you have any other suggestions?"

"There's no need to snap! I was only making conversation!"

"Well, don't! Concentrate on watching the ice, instead of annoying me!"

"Don't you worry. The first sign of a crack and I'm off. I've made more emergency takeoffs than you've blasted rebels!"

"And what about my escape?"

"Hey, you can swim, can't ya?"

Ignoring the droid's feeble attempt at humor, Korda approached the jagged hole in the surface. Nothing about this made sense. The sides of the breach were meters thick, easily strong enough to support a ship as small as the *Whisper Bird*. Why had it cracked the ice?

Sudden movement on the horizon provided the answer. Korda looked up as a jet of hot water erupted into the air with a *whoosh!*

"That's it," he said out loud. "Geysers beneath the ice. If the *Whisper Bird* landed on top of one . . ."

"*What was that?*"

"I wasn't talking to you!" Korda said, shutting off the transmission before the droid could reply. He rubbed the bridge of his nose in frustration. This couldn't be happening.

He had lost the *Whisper Bird* again.

Korda's mind went back to the day when he had first received his orders from Darth Vader.

Get me those maps, Commander. Wild Space belongs to the Empire.

How simple had it sounded back then? Find the Grafs and return with their data. Lord Vader would reward him for a job well done. Who knew what other missions he'd be given, what glory awaited?

Glory. The word tasted bitter on his tongue.

Korda considered turning around and marching back to the ship. Perhaps he would take his anger out on that droid, teach the thing some respect.

But then something caught his eye. He knelt, running gloved fingers across the ice. Yes, there were marks, tiny pinpricks left by ice grips! So at least one of the children had escaped the crash.

He stood and followed the tracks. They were

heading toward a rocky outcrop in the distance. Korda smiled. By the look of the indentations, the child had been running.

Not fast enough.

Korda pulled his field electrotelescope from his pocket. He put it to his eye, immediately picking out movement against the rocks. *There!* He zoomed in just as Lina Graf glanced over her shoulder.

"Got you!"

Korda hurried back to the *Star Herald.* Within minutes he was back on the flight deck, opening the weapon locker.

"Going somewhere?" RX-48 asked.

"The girl is hiding in nearby caves."

"Alone?"

"There was only one set of tracks, but the droid may be with her."

"It can fly?"

Korda checked his blaster, resisting the urge to take the pilot's head off.

"It hovers. Repulsorlift technology."

"Fancy!" RX-48 complained. "What I wouldn't give for a repulsor, but no, I'm bolted to the floor while he floats around without a care in the world. Some droids have all the luck."

"Don't worry," Korda said, clicking two long rods together to make a force pike. "His luck is about to run out."

Korda twisted the shaft, igniting the energy lance at the tip.

"And what should I do while you're off having fun?" RX-48 asked.

"Drop a probe into the water," Korda replied, marching from the flight deck. "We need to find that ship, just in case the maps are still on board."

"Yes, oh, lord and master. Your wish is my command!"

Korda ignored the droid's sarcasm. He stomped down the ramp to the ice and took a deep breath, the cold air filling his lungs. Using

the force pike as a staff, he strode purposefully
toward the island.

This was it. The final hunt!

On board the *Whisper Bird*, Milo and CR-8R
were hard at work. CR-8R had managed to
pump most of the seawater from the ship,
but they weren't out of danger yet. The droid
had insisted that Milo change out of his wet
clothes, hovering around with blankets and
heaters, but things had gone from bad to
worse.

Not long after the hatch was sealed, the
Whisper Bird had come to rest on what Milo
had assumed was the ocean bed. However, it
soon became clear that they had farther to fall.
They hadn't reached the bottom at all but were
perched on the edge of an underwater cliff.
There was no way of telling how many fathoms
of water lay beneath them. All Milo knew was

that even the slightest movement sent the ship rocking. If the cliff face crumbled beneath their weight, all would be lost.

Ideally, Milo and CR-8R should have tried to keep still, but that just wasn't an option. The main power system was down, the *Whisper Bird* operating on emergency batteries alone. Life support was on minimal, the air already becoming stale, and they could barely see. Every light on the ship had fused, but Milo had found the crate of Founder's Day lanterns in storage. Memories of the celebrations came flooding back, but this wasn't the time to reminisce. Milo hung the lights from every hook and doorway, where they swayed gently as the ship tilted back and forth.

Now Milo had another job. He was running around the ship patching up leaks with a can of quick-hardening foam. He wished there was something else he could do. If Lina had been trapped down there with CR-8R she would be up to her elbows in cables, trying to fix the *Bird*'s damaged systems. She had always been a tech head, while Milo was happier out in the natural world. He had an encyclopedic knowledge of plants and life-forms on a dozen worlds, none of which was any use right now.

All he could do was plug holes, Morq hanging from his neck. The little monkey-lizard was terrified, and Milo couldn't blame him.

Suddenly, there was a crackle of energy from the direction of the cockpit.

"Crater?"

Milo sprinted through the ship, trying to ignore the shifting deck beneath his feet.

"Crater, are you okay?"

CR-8R was on his back on the cockpit floor, arms writhing in the air like the legs of a robotic crab.

Milo bent down to help the droid up. "What happened?"

Crater's repulsors kicked in as soon as he was

upright. "I was stupid, that's what. Stupid, stupid, stupid!"

The droid floated up to an exposed control panel. "I tried to bypass the power coupling."

"And that's bad?" Milo asked, watching CR-8R work.

"It is when you can't reset the safety switches. Nothing on this ship is working."

"It is!" Milo argued, trying to look on the bright side. "We have life support. . . ."

"Barely!"

"And you said the shields are holding."

Almost as if it wanted to prove Milo wrong, the *Whisper Bird*'s hull groaned around them.

CR-8R dropped back down to the floor. "For now. I had to divert all remaining power to the particle shield generators. If they fail, the *Whisper Bird* won't be able to withstand the water pressure. We'll be crushed like a tin can!"

"That's a comforting thought," said Milo, his voice wavering as Morq cuddled in closer.

CR-8R ignored him and set about dismantling the computer console. "Even if I could get the propulsion system working, we don't have enough power for the engines. We're stuck here and there's nothing I can do about it!"

Milo had never seen CR-8R so angry. The droid was often irritable and frequently infuriating, but this . . . this was something else.

"Crater, it's all right. . . ." He reached out a hand to touch the robot's arm, as if physical contact would somehow help a machine. CR-8R snatched the shiny limb away. When he spoke again, the frustration had gone from his artificial voice, leaving nothing but sadness.

"It really isn't, Master Milo. I was never programmed for any of this. Your parents activated me to assist in research, not keep you and your sister safe. Ask me a question about the thousands of worlds we've surveyed over the years and I'll know the answer immediately.

Ask me about looking after children, and I know nothing."

This time CR-8R let Milo squeeze his metal hand. "That's not true. You're doing a great job. Mom and Dad would be proud."

Something banged on the ceiling above them. Something outside the ship.

"What was that?" Milo asked.

There was another thump, louder this time.

"Something's out there," Milo whispered, Morq trembling against his neck. "How long did you say the shields will last?"

"I didn't," CR-8R admitted. "Sixty minutes? Maybe more?"

Milo shot a glance at the canopy. The water on the other side was dark. There was no sign of movement.

"Maybe you should take another shot at the propulsion system," Milo suggested. "I'm going to try to contact Lina. Maybe I can boost the signal."

"Good idea," CR-8R agreed, floating out of the cockpit. "Try not to think about sea monsters, or whatever that thing was."

"Thanks," Milo said, activating the comlink. "I won't!"

CHAPTER 5
THE WALL

LINA'S GLOWLAMP shook in her hand. The inside of the cave was pitch-black. Of course it was. She scolded herself for being surprised. What did she expect? It was cold, too, bitterly cold, even through her jacket.

So she was freezing, could barely see where she was going, and had no idea what to do next.

Way to go, Lina. Way to go.

But what choice did she have? Korda was coming. The man who had taken everything from her. First Mom and Dad, then Dil Pexton. Now even the *Whisper Bird* and Milo were gone.

She stopped herself. No, Milo wasn't gone.

He was just trapped. They'd see each other again soon; she was sure of it.

She wasn't going to let Korda win. Not this time.

The cave narrowed into a tight passageway, barely wide enough for her shoulders. She considered turning back but forced herself on. If it was getting too tight a squeeze for a ten-year-old girl, a man the size of Korda would find it impossible.

At least, that's what she hoped.

Maybe he'd get stuck. The idea made her grin. She imagined him scrabbling at the rock, that robotic jaw grinding in frustration. Ha! It would serve him right.

Besides, she'd explored ice caves before. Dad had taken them potholing on Orto Plutonia when she was eight. Mom had stayed on the *Whisper Bird* with Milo while Dad taught Lina how to clamber through the tightest gap and scale sheer walls. Her parents were the best. How many eight-year-olds had been taught how to use ice picks?

There was a noise from behind. Lina froze, listening intently. Something was in the cave with her. An animal? A keejin, or maybe a shyrack? She turned. Light was bouncing off the walls behind her. Not an animal then, unless it had a glowlamp of its own. It had to be Korda. She could hear his footsteps now, getting closer. They were slow, cautious. Korda was trying to keep quiet, to sneak up on her.

She wasn't about to let that happen.

Lina pushed on, trying not to panic. The walls were pressing in, the floor becoming more treacherous with every step. Something caught her arm and she spun around, expecting to see Korda's face leering out of the darkness.

She let out a ragged breath. Her sleeve had just snagged on a rock.

She pulled it free, the silver material ripping.

"I can hear you!"

So much for sneaking up on her! Korda sounded so close, like he could reach out and grab her.

"You can't hide from me, Lina. Not this time."

She didn't want to hide. She wanted to run. She pressed on, not caring if he heard her or not. It didn't matter anymore. Her breath was coming in ragged gasps, her free hand clawing at the rocks to pull her along. How long was this tunnel anyway? At least it was widening now, opening out.

She picked up speed, bouncing off the walls.

Nervously, she glanced over her shoulder, only stopping short when her foot came down on thin air. She threw out an arm, grabbing hold of the wall. It was enough to keep her from falling forward into the great chasm that had opened in the tunnel floor. She wobbled on the edge, stones tumbling into the darkness below. The gap was a meter or two across, but it might as well have been a hundred kilometers for the fear that seemed to grip her heart.

Could she clamber around it? Lina cast her lamp's beam over the walls, revealing nothing but smooth rock, barely any handholds at all. She'd never make it that way. Going back wasn't an option, either, not unless she wanted to run into Korda.

She would have to jump.

She almost laughed at how crazy that sounded. Jump the gap. What if it was wider than it looked? What if she didn't make it across?

There was only one answer to that. She would fall. Fast.

"Lina . . ."

Korda's mocking voice was the encouragement she needed.

Lina backed up, trying to get her breathing under control. She needed to focus on the other side of the crevasse, to imagine herself already there, landing safely. She'd jumped wider streams than this. There was nothing to be scared about. . . .

Other than falling into a bottomless pit, of course.

She couldn't think like that. She tensed, getting ready to run.

One. Two. Three.

Go!

Lina bolted forward and flung herself across the void. She couldn't tell if she cried out as she jumped, or whether she screamed inside. Time seemed to slow down as she flew through the air, her eyes fixed straight ahead.

She wasn't going to make it. What had she been thinking? It was too far. She reached forward. Her foot struck something hard. She fell, expecting to plunge into the abyss, but instead her shoulder made contact with rock. It was painful contact, but she didn't care. She was rolling along the passageway, away from the edge. She'd made it! She'd made the jump!

The glowlamp was still clutched tightly in her hand. She brought up the light to see how far she had leapt. The face of Captain Korda snarled back at her across the chasm. He was on the other side!

Fighting the urge to fling the precious lamp at him, she shot to her feet and ran. The passage was rising steadily now, stalactites reaching down like gnarled fingers. She didn't care. Maybe there was a chamber ahead, somewhere she could hide. She continued to climb, up and up and up until . . .

Lina stopped short, her heart sinking.

No. This couldn't be happening.

There was no chamber at the end of the passage, only a solid wall of ice.

There was nowhere else to go, not to the right or the left. She definitely couldn't go back!

She tried to steady her breathing, looking up. *What would Milo do? What crazy plan would he come up with?*

She flashed the lamp up at the wall. Was that a ledge running across its length, high above her?

Suddenly, she knew *exactly* what Milo would do. He would climb!

The only way is up, Sis!

Holding her lamp between her teeth, Lina delved into her tool belt. There had to be something she could use.

Her fingers brushed against metal. She pulled it out. A pilex bit driver, one of a set of three. She'd lost the biggest when the water had hit the *Whisper Bird*, but this one felt sturdy enough. Her pilex drivers were fitted with a joint halfway along the shaft, so the sharp drill bit at the end could be locked at a right angle to the rest of the tool. She did exactly that, tightening the joint as much as she could. At least it was now the right shape for an ice pick. She could hold it by the handle and hammer the drill bit into the ice to pull herself up.

She searched in her belt for the third bit driver. It was smaller than the first, and the joint didn't feel half as strong when she locked it in place.

Would either of them hold her weight?

There was only one way to find out.

With a grunt, she swung the first bit driver at the wall. The drill bit sunk into the ice and held fast. So far so good. Using the spikes on her boots to push herself up, she swung with her left arm. Again the drill bit held. She climbed hand over hand, remembering how her Dad had taught her all those years before.

That's it, Lina. You can do it!

"I can do it," she repeated, the glowlamp still clamped in her teeth. "I can do it."

The wall wasn't as vertical as she'd first thought. It sloped slightly away from her, which helped, but her arms ached and her legs trembled with fatigue. Soon even the slightest movement became difficult.

Keep going, Lina, she heard her dad say. *Do it for me. Do it for Milo!*

Her right foot slipped and she cried out, the glowlamp dropping from her mouth. She hung there, listening to it clatter to the floor below. How far had it fallen? She must have climbed farther than she thought.

It would be easy to look down. Too easy. But she couldn't risk getting dizzy. She needed to look up. She needed to carry on.

The drill bits hammered into the wall like blaster bolts.

Bang.

Bang.

Bang.

The pain in her arms was unbearable, her shoulders tight, the muscles cramping.

Bang.

Bang.

Bang.

She thought about Milo, how he'd tease her if she fell. *Come on, Lina. Get a move on! You'll never reach that ledge!*

Oh, yeah? We'll see about that!

Bang.

Bang.

The sound of boots crunching on ice far below nearly stopped her in her tracks. She imagined Korda, stepping out of the passage, finding her glowlamp at the bottom of the wall. What was he doing now? Looking up at her? Watching her hang from the ice like a spider? Was he reaching for his blaster, lining up a shot?

Keep going, Lina. Keep going!

She swung her right arm, but was too tired. The drill bit bounced off the ice, the handle slipping from her aching fingers. It tumbled away, and for the first time since she'd started her ascent, Lina looked down.

Korda was there, glaring up at her. She panicked, her feet scrabbling at the ice as she lost her grip on the remaining bit driver.

Lina slid down the slope, screaming all the way. Her gloved hands desperately searched for a handhold, anything to stop her from falling.

And then she was caught by a pair of strong

arms. She looked up to see her terrified reflection staring back at her in Korda's metallic jaw.

"Got you!" he snarled triumphantly.

"Get off me!" she screamed, kicking her legs wildly. "Let me go!"

Korda staggered back, dropping her. She slammed against the ground, winding herself. Fingers grabbed the back of her jacket just as her own hand found something hard on the floor. One of the bit drivers!

She wheeled around, raking the drill bit through the air. Korda stepped back, easily dodging the clumsy attack. He reached for something behind his back. Lina had no idea what until the end of a force pike appeared in front of her face.

She dropped the bit driver and froze.

"Smart girl," Korda snarled. "This pike contains enough power to stun a dewback, let alone a little runt like you."

Lina glared back. "What do you want?"

Korda laughed as if that was the most idiotic question he had ever heard. "Your droid, of course. Or rather, all those maps in his head. Where is he?"

"At the bottom of the ocean," Lina said. "He's gone, along with the maps. Do you understand? The *Whisper Bird*. Milo. Crater. They're all under the ice and there's no way to get them back!"

Something buzzed on her belt. Korda's eyes flashed toward the sound and then widened as a voice crackled over the comlink.

"Sis? Can you hear me? It's Milo. We need your help."

A terrible grin spread across Korda's face. "Did you hear that? Your brother's in need of assistance."

CHAPTER 6
STRANGERS IN THE DEEP

"LINA, PLEASE. Can you hear me?"

Milo flopped back into his seat and let his head fall into his hands. He was trying really hard not to cry. At his feet, Morq nuzzled into his leg and whimpered. Milo reached down and ruffled the monkey-lizard's tuft of red hair. "It's okay, boy. We'll get through to her. Maybe the signal isn't strong enough."

"Or Mistress Lina has moved out of range," CR-8R suggested, hovering into the cockpit.

"Any luck?" Milo asked.

"With the propulsion systems? If you ask me, the *Whisper Bird* will never fly again. I estimate we have roughly thirty minutes before the shields collapse."

"Could we swim to the surface?"

"You'd freeze. I'm afraid I'm quickly running out of—"

The ship bucked and Milo tumbled out of his chair. Morq squealed in alarm, but CR-8R nimbly shot out a manipulator arm to catch his young master.

"Thanks. Was that the cliff?"

Outside, something scraped along the hull. Something very, very long.

"I don't think so," the droid replied.

The *Whisper Bird* rocked again, the noise coming from all around.

"Something's wrapped itself around the ship," Milo said. "Can we get the external sensors working?"

"I'm almost too afraid to look!" CR-8R admitted as he reached for the controls. The entire ship was creaking around them.

"It's like we're being crushed," Milo said, jumping out of the way as a new leak appeared above his head.

"Well, surprise, surprise," said CR-8R with an electronic sigh. "None of the sensors are working. We're as blind as an Ithorian bat!" A sharp scraping noise had joined the creaks and groans. "Now what?"

"It sounds like claws," Milo said. "What *is* it out there?"

CR-8R didn't reply.

"Crater?"

The droid was looking over Milo's shoulder. "Now, don't panic, Master Milo."

"What is it, Crater?"

The droid's voice dropped to a whisper. "Don't look now, but I think we're being watched."

He pointed with a trembling finger. Milo turned and gasped.

A vast unblinking eye was staring at them through the canopy window.

"He's not paying me enough for this," RX-48 complained as he launched a surveillance probe. Lights flashing, the spherical drone hovered down the ship's ramp and headed toward the hole in the ice. RX-48 watched its progress, checking the probe's data feed as it dropped into the water.

"I should be piloting pleasure liners for

the Galactic Tourist Bureau, not freezing my antennae off in the middle of nowhere. I don't know, you crash one tour bus into a space station—"

A buzz from the comlink stopped the droid's moaning. Oh, good, Korda wanted a word. That was all he needed.

He flicked the switch. "Yes, yes, I've launched the probe," he said before the captain could start shouting. "It's on its way to the *Whisper Bird*'s watery grave."

"We need the exact location of that ship," Korda said. *"The boy and the droid are still on board."*

"And what exactly are we going to do when we find it?"

"Rescue them, of course!"

"Rescue them? We shot them down!"

"You shot them down," Korda reminded the droid. *"This is your last chance, droid!"*

The line went dead, leaving RX-48 glaring at the speaker.

"He really is the rudest person I've ever met, and I've worked for Jabba the Hutt!" He flicked a control, activating the probe's floodlights. "I should contact Jabba when this is all over," he added wistfully. "Maybe old slug-face needs a pilot for his sail barge. . . ."

Morq squealed and leapt from Milo's neck to scamper out of the cockpit.

"Morq, it's all right!" Milo called out.

"All right?" echoed CR-8R. "How can you say it's all right. Just look at that thing!"

The giant eye continued to peer at them.

The ship groaned again, the pressure on the hull increasing.

Milo took a step forward.

"What are you doing?" said CR-8R.

"Taking a closer look," Milo replied, nearing the window.

"Isn't it big enough already?"

Milo reached up to touch the canopy. The

creature outside jerked its head back, the
sudden movement rocking the ship again.

It had not one but four eyes, each a different
size, and a long slit of a mouth. Its skin was
milky white and looked incredibly smooth, as if
it were carved from polished marble.

Long fingers appeared, each tipped with
a sharp claw. They raked against the window,
setting Milo's teeth on edge.

"It's trying to get in!" CR-8R said.

"I don't think so," Milo replied. "It's just
curious. It doesn't know what we are."

The creature jolted again. Milo stumbled as
the ship moved and threw out an arm to steady
himself. When he looked up again the creature
was looking over its huge shoulder. Beams of
light were sweeping through the gloom, reaching
down from above.

"It's a probe," CR-8R said, craning his
telescopic neck. "Someone's looking for us!
Thank the Maker!"

But Milo had spotted something else in the

water, illuminated by the probe's searchlights. "Crater, there's another creature out there. Just look at it! It's beautiful!"

"Beautiful? Are you sure?" The droid followed Milo's gaze and fell silent.

The second creature was huge, much bigger than the *Whisper Bird*. It had the same bulbous head and long clawed fingers, but this time they could see its snakelike tail writhing in the water.

"That must be what's around the ship," Milo said. "It wrapped its tail around us."

"What if I electrify the hull?" CR-8R suggested. "We could scare the hideous thing off!"

But Milo wasn't listening. He was watching the creature in the distance. Its body was glowing, colors rippling along its tail.

All at once, the creature that had grabbed the *Whisper Bird* released its grip. The ship pitched forward, and for a moment Milo was convinced they were about to topple over the edge of the cliff.

Then they rocked back, settling into place.

The creature swam back to its mate, its own tail flashing bright orange. The two monsters swam around each other and then back away.

"The probe's frightening them away." CR-8R said, sounding relieved. "Good riddance!"

"No, don't you see it, Crater?"

"See what?"

Milo pointed at the sea creatures. "The

colors on their tails. They aren't random. They're following a pattern."

"All very interesting, but—"

For a machine with an IQ the size of the known galaxy, CR-8R could be very dumb sometimes.

"They're talking to each other!" Milo said, turning to the droid. "Crater, remember those octopoids Dad studied on Mannius Eight."

"Of course I do," CR-8R said. "There's nothing wrong with my memory banks!"

"So how did they communicate?"

"By changing the patterns on their skin! Of course. Your father conducted an intriguing study into the language and vocabulary—"

"Yes, yes, yes." The last thing Milo wanted was a lecture. "Don't you see? That's what *they're* doing. They're communicating using the lights in their tails."

CR-8R stared at him in disbelief. "You're not thinking what I think you're thinking?"

"Perhaps we can talk to them, too, use lights to send them a distress message or something. They may be able to help us!"

CR-8R turned to see the creatures rushing toward the probe. The drone swung around, as if trying to dazzle the advancing monsters with its floodlights. The nearest creature opened its gaping maw, revealing row after row of gigantic teeth. A second later the probe had been swallowed whole!

"Still think they will help?" CR-8R asked.

RX-48 banged one of his rusted pincers against the monitor screen. The probe had stopped transmitting just as things were getting interesting.

"Right when I thought today couldn't get any worse," the droid muttered. "Old chrome-jaw's not going to like this, not one little bit."

The pilot flicked switches and pressed

buttons, anything to reestablish the link with the probe. "What in the name of the Maker were all those colors, anyway? And I'm sure I saw the Grafs' pathetic excuse for a starship."

Still there was no response.

"Come on, come on. What's happened to you?"

The floor creaked behind him. RX-48 sighed and started to turn around.

"Look, before you start yelling, it wasn't my fault. The stupid probe just cut off, and . . ."

The droid stopped talking when he saw a row of blasters pointing toward him. He whirled around, reaching for the pistol he'd taped beneath the controls just in case Korda turned nasty.

Well . . . nastier.

He never got the chance to use it. Blaster fire slammed into RX-48's robot body, disintegrating it on contact.

The droid's metal head bounced once before

rolling across the flight deck to be stopped by a white-booted foot.

"I told you it wasn't my day," RX-48 whined before deactivating forever.

CHAPTER 7
SNOW FIGHT

"GET BACK!" Korda commanded, dragging Lina from the mouth of the cave.

"Were those blasters?" she asked as he pushed her flat against the wall.

"Yes," he hissed, peering around the edge of the rocks. "Snowtroopers. They've found me."

"Found you? They're not *with* you?"

Lina took another look at the man. Suddenly, everything made sense. His unkempt appearance. The battered body armor beneath the furs. "You're not with the Empire anymore, are you? They threw you out!"

Korda whirled around and grabbed her wrist, pulling her close.

"Yes, they threw me out. Because of you and your brother."

"Because you couldn't catch us!"

Lina felt a swell of pride. *They* had done this to him.

Korda let go of her arm. "Imperial High Command discovered that I'd hired a bounty hunter to find you. I was court-martialed, stripped of my rank, and condemned to a life harvesting spice on Kessel."

"But you escaped. . . ."

Korda's top lip curled up in a disgusting mockery of a smile. "I stole the *Star Herald*. A fine ship. A prototype that the Empire obviously wants back."

"But if you're not with the Empire . . ."

"Why come after you?" Korda said, finishing her question.

Lina nodded.

Korda sighed. "Consider it a matter of pride. I'd vowed to recover your parents' maps. I wasn't going to let a little thing like being publicly disgraced stand in my way."

"Plus, you could always sell them to the highest bidder."

Korda looked at Lina with something approaching respect. "You really are smarter than you look."

"Thanks . . . I think."

There was a noise from outside, booted feet approaching the caves.

"How many are there?" Lina asked.

"Snowtroopers? A small section—maybe two or three."

"Then we need to get away."

Korda's hideous grin returned. "I'm done running. It's time to fight!"

Beneath the water, Milo watched as the two creatures swam back and forth in front of the *Whisper Bird*.

"They're going to attack!" CR-8R whined.

"Then we have to stop them."

"How?"

Milo glanced at the lanterns he had strewn all over the cockpit. "Crater, those things can change color, right?"

The droid looked confused. "Yes. Your mother designed the bulbs to flash in time with music. . . ." He paused as he realized what Milo was planning. "It will never work."

Milo wasn't about to be discouraged. "Can you link them to the comms system?"

Muttering to himself, CR-8R set about creating a wireless network between the lights. Milo urged him on, aware that the bizarre sea creatures were swimming closer with every passing second.

"Ready?"

"As I'll ever be," came the droid's reply.

"Try a simple sequence first."

"Like what?"

"I don't know, three flashes of blue, and then one red."

CR-8R pressed a sequence of buttons on the comms console and the lanterns flared to life exactly as Milo had instructed him.

Blue.

Blue.

Blue.

Red.

The response was instantaneous. The two monsters thrashed in the water, almost turning somersaults.

"That certainly attracted their attention," CR-8R said.

"Try again," said Milo. "Three flashes of green."

CR-8R did as he was told.

Green.

Green.

Green.

This time, both creatures propelled themselves

forward, heading straight for the *Whisper Bird*. Milo jumped back, thinking they were going to ram the ship. Then, right at the last minute, they peeled apart. They whooshed past the cockpit, one to the left and one to the right.

When they reappeared a moment later, both tails were a livid purple.

"They're looking angry," CR-8R said. "I hope we didn't just insult their mother!"

Milo ran his fingers through his hair. "That's the problem. We don't have a clue what we're saying. We're probably talking gibberish!"

CR-8R slapped a metallic palm against his forehead. "Of course! I'm such an idiot."

"What is it?"

"We don't know their language, but the computer might. Your father used translation software to understand the Mannius octopoids. If I run the same program . . ."

"We'll be able to understand what they're saying! Yes!"

CR-8R started busying himself with the computer. "There's a chance at least. We just need to keep them talking."

Milo looked through the window. The creatures were glaring angrily at them, their tails now a brilliant scarlet.

"Crater, I honestly don't think that will be a problem!"

Lina held her breath, worried that the sound would give her away. The snowtroopers were almost at the mouth of the cave. Korda was lying in wait, his force pike gripped in both hands. His face was like stone, but his eyes sparkled. It was almost as if he was enjoying himself!

She caught a glimpse of the first snowtrooper. His face was protected by a long fabric mask, black goggles shielding his eyes. The white armor was a perfect camouflage for arctic conditions, an insulating cape hanging from an equipment belt slung around his waist.

The trooper paused for a moment, peering into the cave. Lina shrunk back into the shadows as he continued, ready for action.

Korda sprang without warning, jabbing at the armored man with his force pike. The trooper threw up an arm, deflecting the weapon's glowing tip. Korda responded by reeling around, the other end of his staff finding the snowtrooper's chest. The force of the blow

knocked the trooper onto his back. Korda leapt
back as the snowtrooper brought up his blaster.
A bolt of sizzling energy shot from the barrel
of the rifle, narrowly missing Korda. It slammed
into the roof of the cave. Stalactites rained down
on Korda, but he didn't seem to mind. The force
pike spun in his hand and came down hard. The
snowtrooper's gun clattered from his grasp and
the armored man lay still.

There was no time to celebrate. A second snowtrooper approached the cave, his blaster raised. Before he could fire, Korda threw the pike like a javelin. It stuck the trooper in the chest, discharging in a brilliant flash of light. The trooper collapsed, a wisp of smoke rising from his chest plate. Lina called out a warning. A third armored figure was crouching behind a rock. Blaster shots burned through the air, and Korda barely managed to throw himself out of their path in time. Shielding himself behind the entrance, he pulled out his own blaster. The two men exchanged shots, but Korda's luck eventually ran out. A bolt smashed into the wall beside his head. The captain cried out as he was struck by flying rocks. He went down and didn't get up again.

Lina's hand went to her tool belt as the snowtrooper entered the cave and cautiously kicked Korda in the side. The captain didn't move.

The snowtrooper raised his blaster, ready to fire.

Whatever Korda had done to her family, she couldn't stand by and watch him get shot at point-blank range. Besides, she would be next!

Grabbing her comlink in one hand and a vibropick from her tool belt in the other, Lina stabbed the pick into the transmitter and twisted. An earsplitting shriek filled the cave. The snowtrooper looked up to see stalactites dropping toward him, loosened by the sonic pulse.

He was buried in an instant.

Lina rushed for the entrance. The snowtrooper had been knocked out, but a groggy Korda was trying to dig himself out.

"Lina, wait. Please."

Something in his voice made her stop, a vulnerability she'd never heard before. She knew she should keep running. This was more than Korda deserved, but her conscience continued to nag her.

If she left him injured in the snow, was she any better than Korda himself? And could she rescue Milo without his help?

Hoping that she wasn't making a huge mistake, Lina turned back and offered Korda her hand.

The man gave her a puzzled look. "If I were you, I'd be running by now."

"But I'm not you," Lina said, stopping herself from adding "thank goodness." She needed to get him on her side. "The thing is . . . we need each other."

Korda gave a snort of derision as he pulled himself back to his feet.

"Okay, I'm listening."

"You're on the run from the Empire, just like us, right?"

He nodded, those cold eyes fixed on her.

"You want our maps; I want my brother back. Maybe we can strike a deal."

"I'll help you if you help me?"

"Sounds fair. I've already saved your life, after all."

"Saved my life?" Korda asked, before laughing. It wasn't a pleasant sound. "Your idea has merit, and that *was* a nice trick with the comlink. You're resourceful. I can almost see how you evaded me for so long."

"You're welcome," she replied.

"Don't push your luck, girl. A truce it is, for now. But if you try to escape . . ."

She raised her hands, hoping she wasn't making the biggest mistake of her life. "I won't, I promise."

"Then we better get going," he growled, staggering out of the cave.

"Are you all right?" Lina asked, gingerly stepping over an unconscious snowtrooper to follow Korda onto the icy rocks.

The captain snatched up his force pike. "I've been in worse fights."

She could believe that. Lina glanced back at

the snowtroopers. "Will there be any more like them?"

"What do you think?" he replied, unclipping his comlink to speak gruffly into the transmitter.

"Korda to *Star Herald*. Come in."

There was no answer.

"Arex-Forate?"

"Trouble?" Lina asked.

"Maybe. We need to get back to the *Star Herald*." He turned and sneered at her. "Are you coming . . . partner?"

CHAPTER 8
PARTNERS

LINA HAD IMAGINED an entire battalion of snowtroopers waiting for them as they trudged across the ice, but the frozen sea was empty except for the *Star Herald* itself. She couldn't relax though, imagining blaster fire cutting them down at any moment.

"Are you sure this is a good idea?" she asked, looking around.

"No," came Korda's reply, "but what's the alternative? Wait for those three to wake up?"

Back at the cave, Korda had offered Lina one of the blasters. She'd shaken her head, not wanting to even touch the horrible thing.

He'd shrugged, burying the rifles in the snow.
He had then searched through the troopers'
equipment packs, finding a climbing rope.
Testing its strength, he'd proceeded to tie the
soldiers together. Lina had no doubt that Korda's
impressive knots would hold the snowtroopers
when they eventually came to, but she had no
desire to find out firsthand.

Korda strode ahead, his broad back to
her. She could run, but where would she go?
She'd seen how easily Korda had tossed that

force pike. The weapon had taken down a snowtrooper; what chance would she have?

No, she would have to trust Korda for now. She wondered what Milo would say. She smiled as she imagined his eyes going wide.

Sis, are you crazy?

Maybe she was, but she had gotten them into this mess. Now she would do anything she could to get them out.

"Quiet!" Korda whispered as they crept through the stolen Imperial ship. The *Star Herald* was eerily peaceful, the only sound the gentle thrum of the idling power systems. Despite her better judgment, Lina stayed close to Korda. They slowed as they reached the flight deck, movement obvious beyond the double doors.

Lina stood on tiptoes to look through a round window. A solitary snowtrooper was checking a display on the flight console. He wore the rank insignia of a commander on his chest and stood beside the scorched remains of what had once been an RX pilot droid.

Lina wanted to ask Korda what they should do, but the former officer was watching the trooper like a Drayberian hawk. The question soon became irrelevant as a blaster cocked behind them. A second snowtrooper stood in the corridor, his weapon trained on Korda.

"I have found the captain," the trooper informed his superior as he marched them both through the doors. The commander looked Korda up and down.

"*Former* captain," he corrected, with obvious pleasure. His helmet turned to Lina. "And who is this?"

"Lina Graf, fugitive and rebel," Korda replied coldly. Before Lina could look at the man in shock, Korda grabbed her jacket and pulled her close. "And my prisoner!"

"You lying monga snake!" Lina yelled, struggling against his grip. "So much for being partners."

"Partners?" he said with a cruel laugh. "You're a bigger fool than I thought."

"But you said—"

"I said what I needed to keep you under control. I had enough to worry about without you making a run for it." The glowing end of the force pike hovered near her face, its heat prickling against her cheek. "Now it's too late to run anywhere."

"Hand her over," the commander ordered, but Korda shook his head.

"Her brother and the droid designated Crater are trapped beneath the surface."

"So?"

"Commander, the droid contains information vital to the Empire. Darth Vader himself ordered me to bring it back."

The snowtrooper shifted at Vader's name. "Then I shall recover the data myself."

"I think not. This ship is fitted with a tractor beam. I propose that we fish the *Whisper Bird* out of the water, retrieve the droid, and deliver the information to Lord Vader together."

"Why should I work with a traitor?" the commander asked. Lina thought it was a good question.

Korda smiled. "Because this *traitor* has programmed the *Star Herald* to only respond to my orders. Quite frankly, Commander, you need me far more than I need you."

He smiled again, like a man who had already won. "Do we have a deal?"

CHAPTER 9
THE TRACTOR BEAM

THE *STAR HERALD* hovered above the ice, its engines thrumming. Korda sat in the copilot's seat and checked the data from RX-48's probe.

"There she is!" he announced as the computer pinpointed the *Whisper Bird*'s precise location.

Lina watched helplessly as he turned to the tractor beam controls. The snowtroopers had cuffed her to a chair, but only after removing her trusty tool belt. She pulled against the restraints, but they wouldn't budge. She was trapped and there was nothing she could do about it.

The snowtroopers meanwhile were watching Korda intently, blasters in hand, just in case.

She couldn't blame them. How could she have trusted him? All that talk about a truce had just been an act. Of course it had. The man didn't have a decent bone in his body. How stupid had she been, thinking she could play a slime-toad like Korda at his own game?

As if he could read her mind, the captain turned to her as he flicked a switch. A loud hum filled the air, accompanied by a faint vibration through the deck beneath their feet.

"Tractor beam activated," Korda announced, smirking at Lina in triumph.

Many fathoms below, Milo and CR-8R were unaware of what was happening above the ice. Instead, Milo was cheering as the sea creatures' tails pulsed with blue and yellow lights.

CR-8R looked up from the computer readout. "They seem to be saying hello!"

"Say hello back!" Milo urged. "We need to ask for their help."

The *Whisper Bird* shook, a warning light flashing on the dashboard. Milo grabbed the pilot's chair to steady himself.

"What's that?"

"It appears we've been caught in a tractor beam!"

"The Imperial ship?"

"Sorry, my psychic circuit seems to be malfunctioning today!"

"This isn't the time to be sarcastic!" Milo snapped as the *Whisper Bird* shuddered again.

"No, it's the time to run around screaming! Engaging panic mode!"

"Don't you dare," Milo said, glancing back toward the window. The sea creatures were nowhere to be seen.

"They must have been scared away," CR-8R said.

Milo cried out as the deck seemed to vanish beneath his feet. He crashed forward, the steering column ramming painfully into his side.

CR-8R checked the computer. "I was afraid this would happen. The cliff face is disintegrating in the tractor beam. We're going over the edge!"

"There has to be something we can do," Milo said. Beside him, the comlink started flashing.

"Yes!" he said, hitting the control. "Lina? Is that you? We could really use some good news right now!"

"I'm afraid your sister is otherwise engaged," a silky voice replied over the comlink. *"But don't worry, I have everything under control."*

Milo recognized the voice immediately.

"Korda!" he said.

The *Whisper Bird* lurched again. Now all they could see was the inky darkness of the waters below.

"Grab on to something!" Milo shouted as the ship went over the edge.

"I'm trying!" insisted CR-8R, hanging on to the rear seat.

And then they were free, plunging down. All around, sparks exploded from every computer console, a giant crack appearing in the canopy window. Every leak that Milo had plugged burst open again, and with a frightened howl, Morq scampered into the cockpit and launched himself at Milo.

Milo hugged his pet tight, not knowing what else to do.

"Shields collapsing," CR-8R shouted over the noise. "Master Milo, I'm sorry!"

Milo buried his head in Morq's fur. All he could hear was rushing water, sparking electricity, and cracking transparisteel.

This couldn't be happening! This couldn't be the end!

CHAPTER 10
SELF-DESTRUCT

THERE WAS A JOLT, and the ship stopped falling. Milo opened his eyes, looking around in confusion.

"They did it!" CR-8R announced. "They locked on! We're being lifted back to the surface!"

"Back into Korda's clutches you mean. What do we do?"

"Get captured?" CR-8R offered unhelpfully.

No, Milo would never do that. What had he said on that holo-recording? No surrender?

Ruffling Morq's fur, he looked around, trying to ignore the cracks in the canopy.

And then he saw movement out in the water. Yes! It was one of the sea creatures!

"Crater, do we have enough power to send another message?"

"With the lanterns?" the droid asked. "Barely!"

"Tell them we need their help."

"Those monsters? What can *they* do?"

"I don't know, but we need to do something. We can't let Korda win!"

The *Whisper Bird* broke the surface of the ocean, water cascading from cracks in its hull. Expertly, Korda maneuvered the destroyed craft onto the ice and disengaged the tractor beam.

On the flight deck, Lina sobbed when she saw the state of her parents' ship.

The *Whisper Bird* was a wreck. One of its wings was missing, the hull pitted. It would never fly again.

Korda set down the *Star Herald* and opened the comms channel.

"Milo. Come in. This is Korda."

There was no response. Korda repeated his

demand, but still they heard nothing but static. What had happened to her brother?

Korda turned to the commander. "We need to retrieve the droid ourselves."

The commander shook his head. "No. We'll retrieve the droid. You stay here."

Korda sat back in his chair and spoke, never taking his eyes from the snowtrooper. "Computer, this is Captain Visler Korda of the Imperial Navy. Prime self-destruct, authorization code: Korda alpha gamma nine."

The commander raised his blaster. "What are you doing?"

He was rewarded with another of Korda's smiles. "I did more than reprogram the *Star Herald* when I 'borrowed' her. I also hid several thermal detonators in her drive systems. Either you agree to my terms or I blow her to smithereens."

"You're bluffing," the commander said. "You'll destroy yourself."

"Commander, my reputation is already in

shreds. What else do I have to lose? Let me be a part of this mission and I'll spare the ship. Freeze me out, or double-cross me in any way, and the *Star Herald* will be blown into tiny little pieces. High Command will be furious. They'll probably take it out on your entire unit."

Lina watched Korda as he spoke. If he was bluffing, he was an extremely good actor. Still, he'd fooled her before.

"Very well," the commander finally agreed.

"Excellent," said Korda, rising to his feet. He paused, then added: "One last thing to mention. The thermal detonators are linked to my life signs." He tapped a transmitter on his chest plate. "If anything happens to me . . ."

He left the sentence hanging, but Lina knew what he meant: *Boom!*

Korda's feet crunched on the ice as he marched toward the *Whisper Bird*. The snowtroopers

followed. What idiots they were, believing that nonsense about the self-destruct. He'd known they would fall for it as soon as the commander had swallowed the lie about the ship obeying Korda and Korda alone.

Besides, as if he would destroy himself! No, Korda knew exactly what he was going to do. As soon as he got his hands on the maps, he would dump these half-wits and take to the stars in the *Star Herald*. The maps would bring him a fortune, more than enough to keep the Empire off his trail.

He could never go back. He knew that now. The Empire was behind him, along with all that bowing and scraping to the likes of Vader.

No, Korda was his own man, in charge of his own destiny. Why work for Emperor Palpatine when he could work for himself?

They came to a stop in front of the *Whisper Bird*. Korda raised his comlink to his lips. "Milo. This is your last chance. Lower the ramp."

He waited, but the brat didn't respond. No problem. Who needed a ramp anyway?

Returning the comlink to his belt, Korda turned to the commander.

"Blast an opening in the hull. As big as you want."

CHAPTER 11
THAT SINKING FEELING

LINA FOUGHT AGAINST her restraints as she watched the snowtroopers fire on the *Whisper Bird*. It was no good. She was going nowhere.

Outside, the snowtroopers had done their job. A gaping hole had appeared in the *Whisper Bird*'s stern. Korda was already climbing on board.

"Look out, Milo," she said, as if her brother could hear.

There was a noise from beyond the double doors. Footsteps. Light, scampering footsteps in the corridor outside. Something had gotten inside the *Star Herald*, some kind of wild animal.

She yanked at her cuffs, the metal cutting into her wrists as the chain rattled against the back of the seat.

The noise seemed to stop the creature, whatever it was.

"That's right!" Lina yelled, trying to sound both braver and scarier than she felt. "Run away! Run away!"

She fell silent again, listening intently. The ship was silent. Had she done it? Had the thing gone?

Then the footsteps sounded again, closer than ever. They were running straight toward her.

The doors of the flight deck hissed open and the creature bounded in, squealing at the top of its voice.

Korda wrinkled his nose in disgust as he marched through the *Whisper Bird*. This was the ship that had evaded capture for so long?

Earlier, out on the ice, he had faked grudging admiration for Lina Graf to gain her trust. Now he only felt pity.

How could anyone live like this?

He turned to the commander and raised a finger to his lips. There was a voice ahead, a young boy's.

Milo.

"Come in, please," the boy said. "This is the *Whisper Bird*. We've been attacked by Imperial forces. Please send help."

Korda smiled. No one would hear the call, not this far into Wild Space. He gripped his force pike and crept toward the cockpit. First he'd deal with the boy and then he'd take out the snowtroopers.

It was almost too perfect.

Milo's whining voice continued its desperate plea. "Come in, please. This is the *Whisper Bird*. We've been attacked by Imperial forces. Please send help."

"No one's coming," announced Korda, stepping into the cockpit. Then he froze.

A hologram of Milo Graf flickered in front of the comm unit, a looped recording playing over and over again.

"Come in, please. This is the *Whisper Bird.* We've been attacked by Imperial forces. Please send help."

He had been tricked!

Korda smashed the transmitter with the force pike, the hologram vanishing.

He spun around. "The boy must be hiding somewhere on the ship. Find him."

But the commander was staring like an infant at the lanterns that were draped around the cockpit's cracked canopy. They were pulsing red and purple, the lights following some kind of simple sequence.

"What are they?" asked the commander.

"Who cares?" roared Korda. "Find the boy!"

The commander took a step closer. "They're pointing down to the ice."

Korda went to grab the man's shoulder when there was a rumble, deep below the ship. The *Whisper Bird* shook as huge white arms burst up through the ice. Korda fell forward as the ship toppled. A massive tail, pulsing purple and red, snaked around the *Whisper Bird*, pulling it down.

Pulling it into the water!

Korda shoved at the commander as they plunged beneath the surface. Freezing water flooded the ship, rushing through the hole the

troopers had blasted. It gushed into the cockpit even as the hull buckled beneath the grip of the monstrous tail.

The snowtroopers struggled in the deluge, their heavy armor weighing them down. Korda didn't give them a second glance. Shrugging off his soaked furs he swam through the ship. The walls were collapsing, but he kept going. Visler Korda wasn't going to die on an insignificant moon light-years from civilization!

His lungs screamed for oxygen as he reached the exit, only to find it blocked by the monster's pulsing tail. Black spots appeared in front of Korda's eyes. He was blacking out. He reached for his blaster, fumbling with the holster. Finally, he pulled it free and fired. The shot went wide, striking the hull, but it did the trick. The tail retreated, enough for Korda to squeeze past and kick himself free of the ship.

Sunlight was streaming through the hole in the ice as he propelled himself up. *Not much longer,* he told himself. *Nearly there.*

Something brushed against his foot, but he kicked it away. He needed to keep going. He needed to survive.

Korda broke the surface just as he felt consciousness slip away. He hacked, the sudden pain of breathing air into his tired lungs bringing back his senses.

He couldn't stop. There was no knowing if the thing that had taken the *Whisper Bird* was coming back. He forced himself to the edge of the ice and dragged his aching body out of the water. He lay there for a minute, gasping for breath, wanting to sleep. *No.* He had to stay awake. He was soaked to the skin. It wouldn't be long before hypothermia set in.

Korda lurched to his feet, shivering in the cool air. Ice crystals had already started forming over his eyes, but there was no mistaking the sound that filled his ears.

The *Star Herald* was taking off!

He wiped his eyes clear and moaned as he saw his stolen ship rising steadily into the sky.

He fell to his knees and bellowed as it rocketed toward the clouds.

"No. You can't do this! Come back! Come back!"

In a second the *Star Herald* was gone.

Alone on the ice, Captain Korda threw back his head and screamed.

The crew of the Imperial cruiser scrambled into action as the *Star Herald* blasted into space. They had expected to hear from the snowtroopers, not see the stolen prototype making an escape bid. The captain of the cruiser called for his deputy to prime the tractor beam, but it was already too late. The *Star Herald* stretched and escaped into hyperspace before he even reached the controls.

On the *Star Herald*'s flight deck, Lina slumped back in the copilot's seat. She was silent, as was her brother. The animal in the corridor had turned out to be Morq, Milo and CR-8R following close behind.

Milo explained what they had done as he used one of her tools to remove the handcuffs. "There are these creatures in the sea. We sent them a message, asking them to attack the *Whisper Bird*, just before we got out."

Milo had sacrificed the *Whisper Bird* to escape, to survive.

Lina still couldn't take it in. The *Whisper Bird* really was gone this time.

Their home.

Their last link to their parents.

She began to cry.

"Sis!" Milo said, wrapping her in a hug. She hugged him back, never wanting to let go.

"I'm sorry," she sobbed. "This is all my fault. If I hadn't lied, if I hadn't tricked everyone . . ."

"You didn't know this was going to happen. Besides, you were trying to find Mom and Dad. They could still be around here."

Behind them CR-8R was examining a screen. "I'm afraid not. It appears the Bridgers' lead was a fake. Captain Korda himself sent the message, to lure you here."

"See!" Lina said, breaking away from her brother. "We should never have come. Now we've lost everything. The ship. All our memories of Mom and Dad."

"Maybe not everything," CR-8R said. With a buzz his holo-emitter burst to life. The flight deck was filled with the recording of Lina, Milo, and their parents playing speeder tag.

"Before we escaped, I downloaded everything I could from the *Whisper Bird's* databanks, including most of your holo-recordings."

Both children raced through the hologram to fling their arms around the bewildered droid. Even Morq joined in, cackling wildly.

"Stop it," CR-8R said, trying to bat them away. Then his voice softened. "I'm just glad you're both safe. I know I'm only a grumpy old droid, but I don't know what I'd do without you two. . . ."

"What about Morq?" Milo asked, wiping away his tears.

"Don't push it!" CR-8R said, trying to dislodge the monkey-lizard from his repulsor unit.

Milo laughed, looking around the pristine flight deck. "I guess we do have a new ship. This thing is seriously cool."

"And wanted by the Empire!" Lina pointed out.

Milo shrugged. "So are we!"

"There's something else," CR-8R said, turning back to the console. "Captain Korda hacked into the Imperial communication network."

"Why would he do that?" Milo asked, peering at the screen.

"Probably so he could keep an eye on official channels," Lina suggested.

"Exactly," agreed CR-8R. "He was looking for any mentions of you or your parents. And he found this."

A picture appeared on the screen. It showed a man and a woman. The image was fuzzy and indistinct, but Milo recognized them right away.

"That's Mom and Dad! Where are they?"

Lina swung herself into a chair and hit a button. Data scrolled across the bottom of the picture. "According to this they've been taken to a planet on the very edge of Wild Space."

"It appears to be some kind of Imperial mining colony," CR-8R told them. "The world is one your parents visited, before you were born."

"Really?" Milo said, peering at the screen. "What is it?"

"One of the first planets they ever mapped. Its name is Agaris!"

EPILOGUE

RHYSSA GRAF stumbled as they were
marched from the Imperial shuttle. Her husband
caught her, and she looked up into Auric's face.

He looked so gaunt, his skin like paper.

She hated to think how *she* looked.

"Move," ordered a stormtrooper, prodding
her in the back. She allowed herself to be
pushed across the hangar and into a dark,
low-ceilinged corridor. Auric held her hand,
their fingers intertwined.

Condensation settled on Rhyssa's skin.
The air on the planet was damp and clammy.
When they were flying in, the place had looked

familiar, although she had no idea why. Rhyssa was having trouble recognizing anything these days. The air in the tunnel was thick with moisture, stinking of mold and rotting vegetation.

They were shoved into a room. It was almost completely bare, except for a table and chairs.

A gloved hand grabbed her shoulder, pushing her down in a seat. They sat in silence, flanked by two stormtroopers, waiting for goodness knew what.

Eventually, a door slid opened and a tall man strode in. His uniform was immaculate, his hands clasped tightly behind his back. His hair, gray at the temples, was slicked back, and his cadaverous face was dominated by a long hooked nose.

The man's sudden appearance had an immediate effect on their guards. The stormtroopers snapped to attention, standing just a little bit taller in his presence.

Who *was* this man?

The newcomer paused opposite them for a moment before pulling out a chair. He sat, smoothed out his coat, and leaned forward on the desk.

Rhyssa couldn't stop staring at his eyes. They were like two black holes, drawing her in.

"Welcome to Agaris," he finally said. His voice was clipped, cultured. He looked at them

both, his thin lips turning up at the corners. Rhyssa's skin crawled. It was like watching a snake trying to smile.

"My name is Wilhuff Tarkin," the man continued. "I need to talk to you about your children."

TO BE CONTINUED IN
STAR WARS
ADVENTURES IN WILD SPACE
Book Six: THE RESCUE